CONCORDIA LUTHERAN SCHOOL
4663 Lancaster Drive NE
Salem, Oregon 97305
503/393-7188

TRY AGAIN
SALLY JANE

Library of Congress Cataloging-in-Publication Data

Diestel-Feddersen, Mary.
  Try again, Sally Jane.

  (A Quality time book)
  Summary: Sally Jane's attempts at roller skating
are failures until animal friends encourage her to try
again until she succeeds.
  [1. Failure (Psychology)—Fiction. 2. Roller
skating—Fiction. 3. Animals—Fiction] I. Ashby,
Yvonne, ill. II. Title.
PZ7.D5735Tr 1987   [E]   86-42810
ISBN 1-55532-175-5
ISBN 1-55532-150-X (lib.bdg.)

North American edition first published in 1987 by
Gareth Stevens Children's Books
1555 North RiverCenter Drive, Suite 201
Milwaukee, Wisconsin 53212, USA

First published in Australia by Era Publications.

Typeset by A-Line Typographers, Milwaukee.
Editor: Mark Sachner
Design: Laurie Shock

TRY AGAIN
SALLY JANE

Story by Mary Diestel-Feddersen
Pictures by Yvonne Ashby

Gareth Stevens Children's Books
MILWAUKEE

Sally Jane was roller-skating
for the first time.
And she was headed straight
for the pond.

"Look out! I can't stop!"

4

Splash!
Into the pond she went.

"Why won't these skates go
where I want them to?" she gurgled.
"I'll **never** learn how to skate."

Sally Jane scrambled up
onto the bank.
She was wet from the top
of her head
to the tips of her skates.

"I'd rather be cleaning
my room!" she said to herself.

Just then, a big green frog
shot out of the pond.

"My toe!" sobbed the frog.
"Can't you be careful?
You squashed my toe!
See what you've done?"

Sally peeked at the frog's toe.
Now she felt even worse.

"I'm *so* sorry," Sally Jane said.
"I really am."

Sally Jane thought of the other kids,
twisting and turning and stopping.
They made skating look like a breeze.

"Skating isn't as easy as it looks,"
she sighed.

"Not **easy**?" croaked the frog.
"What is? Look at what **I** had
to learn how to do. Jump! Dive!
Eat flies!
Do you think **that** was easy?"

15

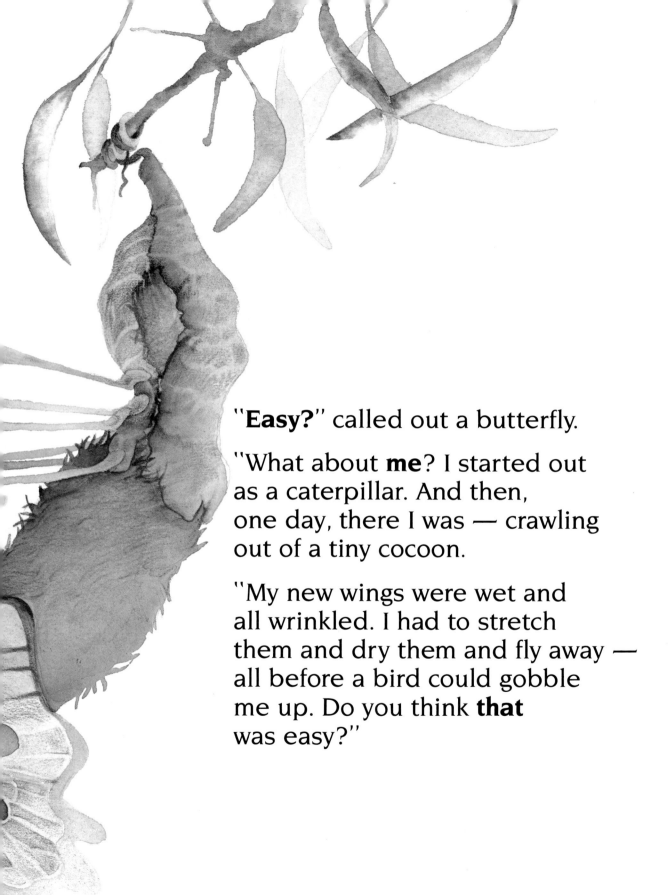

"**Easy?**" called out a butterfly.

"What about **me**? I started out
as a caterpillar. And then,
one day, there I was — crawling
out of a tiny cocoon.

"My new wings were wet and
all wrinkled. I had to stretch
them and dry them and fly away —
all before a bird could gobble
me up. Do you think **that**
was easy?"

"**Easy?**" squawked a pink flamingo.

"How does this sound? I had
to learn to balance on one
leg — and **no** bellyflopping
into the water. Do you think
that was easy?"

19

"**Easy?**" cried a chameleon.

"Let me tell **you**. I had to learn
to change **color**. That's how I hide.

"Once a hungry hawk chased me
into a tree, and I turned green!
A green chameleon in a brown tree!
I changed to brown again quickly.
I saved myself from becoming a meal.
But do you think that was **easy**?"

"**Eas-s-sy**?" hissed a snake.

"Did **you** learn to shed **your** skin as you grew? Once I forgot to grow new skin before shedding the old. I s-s-slid along on my bare bottom for a week! Do you think that was **eas-s-sy**?"

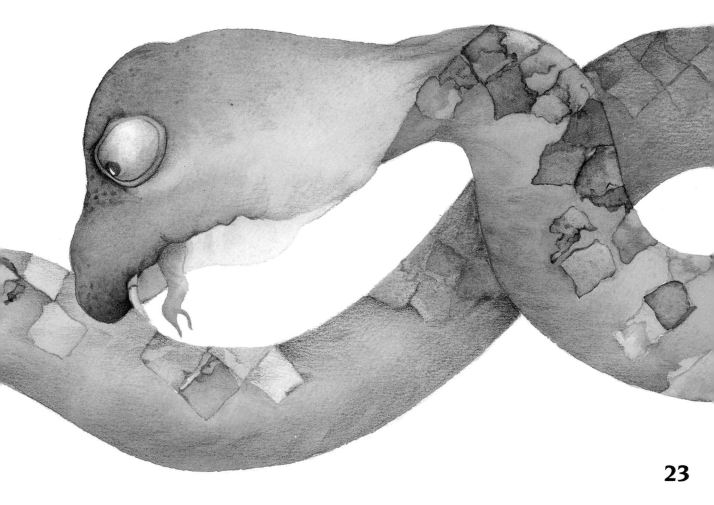

"Wow!" cried the frog.
"What are these rolling things
on your feet? They must have been
hard to grow!

"What can you do with them?"

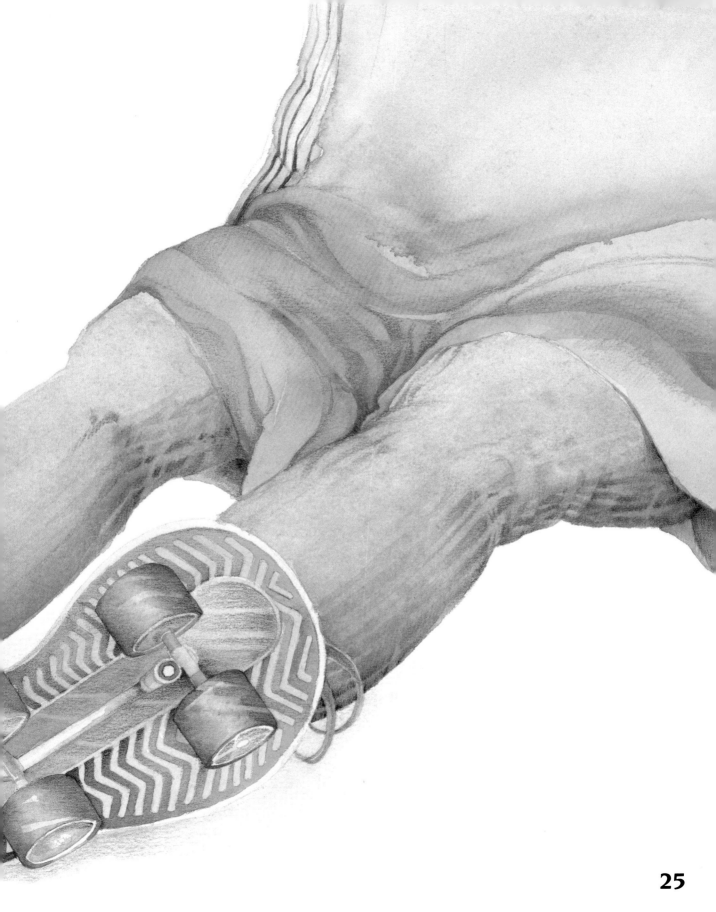

"My skates?" laughed Sally Jane.
"Not much, I'm afraid.

"If only they'd go where
I want them to go," she sighed.
"I could whiz down the street.
I would twist and turn and stop.
But it's not easy to do!"

"Not **easy**?" cried out
all the animals.
"Then **try again, Sally Jane**!"

Sally Jane skated.
She whizzed down the street.
She twisted. She turned.
And she stopped.
She made the skates go
where *she* wanted them to.

"You've got it!" called out
the pink flamingo.

"Hooray!" cheered the chameleon.
"Go, Sally, go!"

"Keep skating!" said the snake
and the butterfly.

"Yee-oww!" cried the frog
as she skated by.

"She's done it again!
Now she's squashed my other toe!"